S.J. Warren

Two Bas-Reliefs of the Stupa of Bharhut

S.J. Warren

Two Bas-Reliefs of the Stupa of Bharhut

ISBN/EAN: 9783337385200

Printed in Europe, USA, Canada, Australia, Japan

Cover: Foto ©Andreas Hilbeck / pixelio.de

More available books at **www.hansebooks.com**

TWO BAS-RELIEFS

OF THE

STUPA OF BHARHUT

EXPLAINED BY

Dr. S. J. WARREN,

GYMNASII RECTOR, DORDRECHT.

LEIDEN. — E. J. BRILL.

1890.

GRATEFULLY AND RESPECTFULLY

DEDICATED TO

Dʳ. J. H. C. KERN

ON THE 26th ANNIVERSARY

·

OF HIS SANSKRIT PROFESSORSHIP

IN THE

·

UNIVERSITY OF LEIDEN.

TWO BAS-RELIEFS OF THE STUPA
OF BHARHUT.

Among the numerous sculptures on the railings and pillars of the Bharhut stūpa, that magnificent Buddhist monument of which General Cunningham has given in his precious work [1]) a minute description and beautiful photographs, many bas-reliefs are illustrations of scenes taken from the Jatakas, stories from previous existences of the Buddha Gautama. Most of those bas-reliefs have inscriptions and as, moreover, the scenes they represent are on the whole very characteristic, the Jataka illustrations have been, for the greater part, identified by Cunningham himself, and, after him, by Rhys Davids [2]), with the Jataka story in the Pali collection which they illustrate. Since 1880, the date of Rhys David's book, Vol. III and IV of Prof. Fausböll's edition of the Jatakas [3]), have appeared, containing 210 stories, by which it is possible to give a text to others of those sculptured illustrations of the tales that have flowed more than twenty centuries ago from the mouth of the great Master.

---

1) The Stupa of Bharhut: A Buddhist monument ornamented with numerous sculptures illustrative of Buddhist legend and history in the third century B. C. by Alexander Cunningham. London 1879.

2) The Jataka Stories. Translated by Rhys Davids, Vol. I. Trübner's Oriental Series. 1880.

3) The Jataka together with its commentary for the first time edited in the original Pali by V. Fausböll. Vol. III 1883. Vol. IV 1887.

On the following pages I have endeavoured to explain two of those bas-reliefs.

The first bears the inscription: *Kinara Jataka*. General Cunningham gives the following notice, page 69:

12. Kinara Jataka.

„This small bas-relief is unfortunately broken, so that the lower halves of the three figures are wanting; but there can be no doubt that the two standing figures are intended for Kinnaras, male and female, in accordance with the title of the Jataka.

The Kinnara was a fabulous being [1]), the upper half of whose body was human, and lower half that of a bird, and the big leaves or feathers which go round the bodies of the two standing figures, must have separated their human bodies from their bird legs.

„In a list of the 550 Jatakas of Ceylon, kindly furnished to me by Subhûti, there is only one in which the name of Kinnara occurs. This is the Chandra Kinnara Jataka, which agrees with the Bharhut bas-relief in limiting its actors to a Raja and a pair of Kinnaras, male and female. The following is a brief summary of the story made from Subhûti's translation of the Jataka."

This story is now published in Vol. IV of Fausböll's edition. It is N°. 485, and may be condensed thus: A hunting raja sees, himself unseen, a pair of Kinnaras; he shoots the Kinnara and endeavours to seduce the Kinnarî. She escapes; he goes away and Saka revives the Kinnara.

Cunningham ends his notice with these words:

„If this is the same as is represented in the Bharhut bas-relief, then the sculptured version differs from the Pali legend of Ceylon in making the pair of Kinnaras dance before the Raja of Benares while he is seated on a chair or throne."

---

1) *Tireedânagatâ* i. e. animals, they are called Jataka IV, 442.

It is clear that the Candakinnarajataka can not be con-
nected with this sculpture. There is in the whole story no
scene corresponding to the illustration.

I take the bas-relief to be an illustration of the Bhallatiya
Jataka, n°. 504 of Fausbölls edition, told by the Lord to
their royal highnesses Pasenadi (Prasenajit), King of Kosala,
and his queen-consort (*aggamahesī*) Mallika.

This Mallika was the only daughter of a garland seller in
Savatthi, the residence of Pasenadi; she was young, fair
and pious. In consequence of a gift to the Buddha she had
been exalted to the high position of queen-consort [1]).

That she is thus suddenly raised in rank causes in her
fits of pride and now and then a quarrel with the King;
but otherwise she is an amiable, modest and faithful wife.
Therefore the Lord Buddha loves her and does take to heart
the quarrels between the royal couple and tells many charm-
ing tales in order to reconcile or to amuse them.

Thus he has told *Mallikam devim arabbha*, concerning the
queen Mallika, the Sujatajataka (306), the Kummasupinda-
jataka (415) and the Bhallatiyajataka (504). Of the lastnamed
a faithful translation is given here.

The introduction is almost the same as in 306:

This story was told by the Lord in Jetavana concerning
Mallika devi.

Once she had a quarrel with the king, a *sayanakalaho* or
sirivivado, that is a bedchamber quarrel.

Annoyed the king took no notice of her any more.

She thought »Surely our Master the Buddha doesn't know
that the king is angry with me."

The Lord heard of the event. Next day he went with
his monks a begging his food in the city and came to the
palace. The king, coming to meet him, took his bowl from

him, begged him to enter the palace and let the monks seat themselves. After having served them with sweet and savoury food he sat down near to them.

Said the Lord: »Why doesn't the queen appear?" The king answered: »She is maddened by the pride of her prosperity." Quoth the Lord: »In a former time, o king, when you were born as a *kinnara* and were separated from your *kinnarī* one night you have repented it seven hundred years." At the request of the king he now tells what happened during a former life.

The introduction to 806 relates the same story in terms somewhat different from those used above. The king is so angry on account of the same cause that he even ignores the existence of the queen. The Lord, hearing the royal pair does not live on friendly terms, thinks: „I will reconcile them with each other", goes to the palace, but, before accepting any food, asks where the queen is. „Don't mind her (says the king); her success has made her presumptuous." „Sire, says the Lord, you have raised her so high your self; having raised a woman so high, you must also bear with her faults." The king sends for her and the Lord exhorts them to peace and concord, by telling the Sujatajataka, which, however by no means so pretty, has the same effect as the Bhallatiyajataka, the translation of which is as follows:

One day the king of Benares, Bhallātiya by name, thought: »I should like to eat meat of deer roasted on coals." After having entrusted the affairs of government to his ministers, he left the city, armed with five sorts of weapons, and followed by a pack of excellently trained dogs. Thus going along the Gangā, he went up the Himavat mountains. When he could not ascend higher there, he followed a rivulet, that flowed into the Gangā, killed many antelopes, bears etc., and having eaten meat, roasted on coals, he climbed up a hill. At the foot of the hill flowed a beautiful rivulet, of which the water, when swollen, reached to the breast, when shallow, to the knees. A multitude of various fishes and tortoises swam in it; the sand along the banks glittered like silver; on either shore stood, bent by the burden of flowers and fruits, various trees, full of birds and bees, intoxicated by the fragrance and the juice of the flowers and fruits, while various beasts, antilopes etc., sought a shelter in the shade of the trees. On the banks of that delicious stream the king saw two *kinnaras*, who, embracing and kissing each other, wailed and wept. He thought: »I will ask those *kinnaras* why they weep," and looking at his dogs, he snapped his fingers, at which the well trained noble animals crept into the bushes, and crouched down on the ground. When he had seen that they were gone, he deposed his bow and quiver and other weapons near. a tree on the earth, and, having stolen softly up to the *kinnaras*, he asked »Why are both of you crying?"

The *kinnara* said nothing, but the *kinnari*, conversing with the king, spoke the following stanza;

Kinnari. Mallagiri, Pandaraka, and Tikuṭa, along those cool rivers do we sojourn. Animals and men, o hunter, know us as *kimpurishas.*

King. Most piteously are ye wailing, although the beloved is embraced by his beloved. I ask thee, that art endowed with a human body, why are ye weeping here so sadly in the wood?

(This stanza is twice repeated with the only change from *weeping* to *lamenting* and *mourning*).

Kinnari. Against our will we passed a single night separated from each other, o hunter, thinking of each other; remorseful we mourn for that single night: that night can not return.

King. That single night for which you mourn as for lost money or a dead father — I ask thee, fair creature, how did it happen that you passed that night separated?

Kinnari. The rapid stream, you see, whose rocky shores are covered with various trees, my beloved once crossed in the rainy season, believing that I followed him.

And I myself gather *onkolakas*, and *atimuttas*, and *sattalis* [1]): my lover shall wear a wreath of flowers and I, myself covered with flowers, I will go to him.

And gathering flowers from blossoming riceplants, I make a garland: my lover shall wear etc.

And gathering flowers from a flowering *sal* tree, I make a heap; this shall be a couch for us, on which to lie down to night.

And careless I crush with a stone aloe and sandelwood; my beloved's body shall be perfumed, and, with a perfumed body I shall go to him.

But the water came quickly, carying along my flowers and garlands; the river was filled and could not be crossed [2]).

Thus we stood each on a bank, seeing each other; and now we wept, then we laughed and slowly that night crept.

And early in the morning, as soon as the sun had risen, we crossed the shallow river, huntsman, and, embracing each other, we, both of us, wept and laughed.

Within three years 700 years have elapsed since we spent here a night, separated from each other, huntsman; your life lasts but a hundred years; how can you dwell here without your beloved?

King. And your life, how long does it last? If you know,

---

1) The original has many other names of flowers.

2) There is a very fine poem by J. Ingelow, translated by our great poet Potgieter: „Gescheiden" in which also two lovers are separated by a river. But the conception of the modern poet is loftier, and moreover symbolical.

by tradition or by the report of the ancients, tell me the time of your life [1]).

Kinnarī. Our life lasts a thousand years, and during it we know no hideous sickness; few are the sufferings, more numerous the joys; ever loving, we leave life.

Having heard this the king thought: »These beings, which are but animals, mourn sevenhundred years for the separation of a single night, while I dwell in the woods, having left the delightful pleasures of my great kingdom of 300 *yojanas.* Alas! I am a fool!" And he returned to Benares, told his ministers what had happened to him, and passed his life in giving gifts and enjoying pleasures.

Then thee Lord spoke two stanzas:

»Having heard this from not human beings, rejoice and quarrel no more, lest remorse torment you, like the kinnaras that single night."

And the queen Mallikā, having heard the Lord's exhortation, arose from her seat, and raising her joined hands to her forehead, she praised the Lord, and spoke the last stanza:

»With a believing mind, I hear thee, pouring forth many blessfull words; speaking, o Lord, thou dispels my pain. O happines bringing *samana.* live long for us!"

And the king of Kosala lived thenceforth in peace with his queen.

Jataka 306 has also been told by the Lord, with the same intention and the same effect, whence it may be perhaps inferred, that, by the editors themselves of the Jatakabook, the pious fiction, that the Lord Buddha should have told all those tales on particular occasions, was itself considered a fiction and treated as such.

---

1) I am not quite sure about the meaning of the text.

It is clear that this Bhallaṭiyajataka is a tale, better fitting to the bas-relief, than the Kinnarajataka· (485), in which the king kills the Kinnara unawares, and the Kinnari escapes, so that, in not any part of the tale, the Kinnara couple stands quietly before the calmly seated Raja. The only difficulty is the title, but it is not paramount, as the titles, engraved on the sculptures, often differ from those of the corresponding Pali stories. The Naga jataka, for example (Cunningham, Plate XXV), is the same as the Kakkaṭa (267) of the Pali collection; Hamsaj. (Plate XXVII) is called in the Palibook Naccajataka (32).

Even the Kinnarajataka in question is there called Canda-kinnaraj. The Bhishaharaniyaj. (Plate XLVIII), not identified by Cunningham, has in the Ceylonese collection the title of Bhisajataka (488).

The second bas-relief also, which I will now explain, bears a quite different title from the corresponding Jataka story.

The photograph is given by General Cunningham on plate XLVI and is very fine, very clear and characteristic. Cunningham gives the following description:

„The actors in this scene are a holy Rishi, with a pair of dogs and a pair of cats. The simple title of *Uda Jataka* does not occur in the long list of the 550 Jatakas of Ceylon; but there is an *Udasa* or *Udacani J.* and an *Uddala J.*, one of which may possibly be the subject of the Bharhut sculpture. The Rishi is seated on the ground with his waterbowl and a basket of food near him. Before him is a pool of wa-ter, stocked with fish. On the bank a pair of cats are qua-relling over the head and tail of a fish, and beyond them are two dogs, one trotting joyfully off with a bone, and the other sitting down disappointed, with his back turned to his luckier rival. — This story ought to be identified at once by any one possessing a complete copy of the 550 Jatakas. The title of *Uda Jataka* means simply the „Water Birth", but I suspect that the name has been unintentionally shortened by the sculptor."

It is quite true what Cunningham says that „any one possessing a complete copy ought to identify at once the story"; so striking is the illustration, that I recognised it at first sight.

The tale is called, in the Pali collection, the *Dabbhapupphajataka* (400). Here follows the translation.

In olden times, when Brahmadatta reigned at Benares, the Bodhisat was a treegod, on the bank of a river. Then a jackal, Deceitful was his name, dwelt there on that bank. Now one day his wife said to him: »Dear Sir, a *dohalo* ¹) has taken hold of me: I long to eat a fresh goldfish." Quoth the jackal: »Be easy, my dear, I will bring thee a goldfish." Having spoken these words, he strolled along the bank of the river, through the creeping plants. Just at that moment, Deepgoing and Riverbankgoing, two otters (*udda* ²) Skrt. उद्र *udra*), were standing on the bank, prying for fish. And Deepgoing saw a big goldfish; quickly he sprung into the flood and seized the fish by the tail. But the big fish dragged him along.

Therefore he called his friend to the rescue, crying: »Riverbankgoing, my dear friend, rescue me! I have taken a big fish, but he drags me along with force."

On hearing this the other spoke the second stanza: »Deepgoing, my dear, take hold of him strongly; I shall draw him out of the water, as a *goruḍabird* a serpent."

---

1) *Dohalo* is the craving desire of a pregnant woman. The *dohalas* play a great part in the tales. In Jataka 501 a queen sees in a dream a goldcoloured deer. Awaked she thinks: „If I say to the king that I have seen it in a dream, he will take no heed of it; but when I say it is a dohalo he will do his uttermost to procure it," and she acts accordingly with the best effect.

2) The title on the basrelief is *Uda*, as consonants are not doubled.

And together they drew the fish on shore and killed him.

But as they were about to divide their prey, they quarrelled and so they sat there, not knowing how to divide it rightly. Just at that moment the jackal appeared on the bank. Seeing him, both turned to him and spoke the third stanza:

»Strife has arisen betwixt us, o Kuçagrasscoloured, listen to me; Appease our strife, Sir, let our quarrel be ended!'.

Having heard those words the jackal said:
»I have always been just, many cases have been decided by me; I will appease your strife; this quarrel shall be ended."

And dividing the fish, he said:
»The tail is for Deepgoing, the head for Riverbankgoing, the middle part shall be for me, the just."

Having thus divided the prey, he said: »Don't quarrel any more, but eat the head and the tail," and, having seized the middle part with his teeth, he ran away. Sadfaced they sat there, as if they had lost a thousand coins and spoke the sixth stanza:

»For many a time there would have been food, if we had not quarrelled; Now the jackal robs us of the fish without head and tail."

The jackall was very glad in his mind, as he thought: »To day my wife shall eat a goldfish," and he ran to her. Seeing him she said, rejoicing:

»As a noble king would rejoice, having taken a kingdom, So I to-day rejoice, seeing my lord fullmouthed."

And asking him in what way he had got hold of his prey: »How hast thou, that art landborn, taken a fish in the water? Answer my question, sir, how hast thou seized it?"

And the jackal, telling her in what way he had gotten hold of the fish, said thereupon:

»By quarrelling they grow poor, by quarrelling they lose

their wealth; The otters have lost their prey by strife, eat
thou, Deceitful, this fish."

I think, it can't rationally be disputed that the bas-relief
is an illustration of this tale, and that the cats and dogs
of General Cunningham are otters and jackals. I must con-
fess I can't see disappointement on the face of one of the
jackals. As he is the bigger of the two, I think he is the
he-jackal, that, having given the fish to his wife, casts a
departing glance at the deceived otters. The human figure
on the bas-relief is, beyond doubt, a Rishi, and not a *devata*;
but that difference is of no importance because the Bodhisat,
as in more Jatakas, where he is a treegod, takes no part
in the action, but is only a figurant, a κωφὸν πρόσωπον.

I have nowhere met with a downright imitation of this Játaka
story. Only the wellknown fable of La Fontaine, *L'huître et
les plaideurs* (X, 9), seems to be a far-off echo of it [1]). La
Fontaine has taken it from Boileau, who has versified it in
his second Epître. Unfortunately I have not been able to
discover whence Boileau has taken it. He himself says: „Un
jour, dit un auteur, n'importe en quel chapitre", and the
only annotator, I have been able to consult, says, with the
same *nonchalance*, that „elle est tirée d'une ancienne comédie
Italienne". Likewise Eugène Lévêque, in his uncritical work:
„Les mythes et les légendes de l'Inde et la Perse dans Aris-
tophane etc.", speaking of this fable and comparing it inju-
diciously with a buddhist Avadana [2]), translated from the
Chinese by St. Julien (Avadâna LXXIV), says flippantly:

---

1) Imitations of this fable are to be found in French reading-books.

2) This Avadâna, „La dispute des deux démons", is quite the same story as that
of king Putraka and the two men with the magic cup, staff, and pair of slippers,
told by Somadeva in his first book, and bears but a remote likeness to the Jâta-
kastory. It reminds on of the Dutch proverb, versified by Jacob Cats: „Twee hond-
"n vechten om een been, Een derde loopt er ras mee heen."

„Pour arriver à La Fontaine, la Dispute des deux Démons a été transformée dans un fabliau français ou italien".

Of the same origin as La Fontaine's fable is perhaps the story of the two cats, which, having stolen some cheese, quarrel about the division of their prize, refer the matter to a monkey to act as arbitrator and are cheated by their judge [1]).

This Jataka contains nine stanzas; moreover, in the epilogue the Lord himself, as Abhisambuddha, speaks a tenth stanza; nevertheless it is classed in the seventh section (*sattanipāta*).

It is also worth remarking that the moral, pointed out by the Lord in the last stanza, does not agree with the moral of the introductory story.

The stanza says: „So, where strife arises between men, they run to a just man: he teaches them what is right; then they lose their wealth; and the king's treasure increases."

In the introductory story a tale is told of the greedy priest Upananda. It is a fictitious tale, partly composed of a story told in the Mahavagga (VIII, 25 p. 800), where Upananda three times accepts a lot of clothes from some monks who are dividing clothes, presented to them at the end of the *vassa*. The Buddha, on hearing of the bad conduct of Upananda, disapproves of it, and reproves him, ending with the solemn formula: *āpatti dukkaṭassa*.

Out of this Mahavagga chapter and the Jataka story itself the Introductory story (*paccuppannavatthu*) is composed, not very artistically indeed [2]). In it Upananda is represented as a monk, who, exhorting his fellowmonks to simplicity

---

1) I have met with this fable in Chambers's National Reading book, III part, where it is given without the name of the author.

2) E. g.: An in the Jataka story occurring expression (*valliyā pāde palibuddhitvā*) is somewhat clumsily adopted in the Introduction.

and modesty, so that his hearers throw away their fine clothes and wear tattered garments (as monks ought to do), procures for himself a good many fine robes and finally cheats two old priests, who have invoked his aid, as the otters that of the jackal. The Lord, hearing of his hypocrisy and robbery, says: „Upananda has not, o monks, acted according to moral duty; a monk, who preaches about their duties to others, ought in the first place to act up to his principles, and then admonish others.

„Let each man apply himself first to what is propre;
Then let him teach others; thus a wise man will not suffer."

(Dhammapada vs. 158)

Not now for the first time, o monks, in a previous existence also has Upananda been covetous and greedy; neither does he rob only now these monks of their property; formerly also did he do so."

Then he tells the Birth Story, in concluding which he identifies Upananda with the jackal, the two old monks with the otters and himself with the tree deity.

The two Jataka stories, spoken of above, are very old stories, as is testified by their being cut in stone on the Bharhut monument, the age of which is assigned by General Cunningham to the Asoka period, somewhere between 250 and 200 B. C. There are many stories in the Pali collection, which, though not sculptured on that monument, date also at least from the third or fourth century B. C., as they are already found (not yet in the form of Jatakas) in the older texts, e. g. the *Dighitikosalaj.* (371) in Mahavagga X, 2, the *Tittirij.* (37) in Cullavagga VI, 6. As in the case of the *Uda-* or *Dabbhapupphaj.*, the introduction of many other stories has been taken from the Mahavagga or other old textbooks, e. g. that of the *Kamaj.* (467) is a fine paraphrase of two *suttas* from the *Suttanipata*, viz. *Dhaniyasutta* and *Kāmasutta*. It seems, indeed, that the authors of the Introductory stories had embraced the doctrine of „Je prends mon bien où je le trouve", even from profane texts. Thus the introduction of the 118th Jataka is an imitation of the plot of the drama in which the love of Carudatta and Vasantasena is exhibited with great poetical force. It is true, one of the *dramatis personae* is a Buddhist monk: our Buddhist authors were thus in good company.